Castle

POLICE

Chemist

Florist

Hospital

Post Office

This is Nurse Nancy. She is always
neat and tidy and she works very
hard looking after the patients
at Story Town Hospital.

A catalogue record for this book is available from the British Library

Published by Ladybird Books Ltd
80 Strand London WC2R 0RL
A Penguin Company

10

© LADYBIRD BOOKS LTD MMI

LADYBIRD and the device of a Ladybird are trademarks of Ladybird Books Ltd

Printed in Italy

Little Workmates

Nurse Nancy

by Ronne Randall

illustrated by Emma Dodd

Ladybird

"I feel as fit as a fiddle this morning," said Nurse Nancy to her dog, Patch. "It's going to be a busy day!"

On her way to the hospital,
Nurse Nancy saw Builder Bill
mending the library roof.

"That roof will soon be as fit
as a fiddle, Bill!" she called.

Nurse Nancy's first stop
was at the Baby Clinic.

Mr and Mrs Baker had
brought their baby, Cherry,
in for a checkup.

Nurse Nancy laid Cherry carefully on the weighing machine...
She had grown a lot!

Then Nurse Nancy listened to Cherry's chest with a stethoscope. She could hear her heart going,

Ka-thump! Ka-thump!

"She's as fit as a fiddle!" said Nurse Nancy.

Soon it was time for Nurse Nancy to pay a visit to the ward.

She checked Mrs Groan's pulse and took her temperature...

Then she gave Mr Grumble
his medicine.

Suddenly Nurse Nancy
heard an ambulance...

MEE-MA!
MEE-MA!

That meant
there was
an emergency...

Nurse Nancy ran to see who had been brought in.

It was Builder Bill! He had hit his thumb with a hammer and hurt himself! He was looking very unhappy.

"Don't worry, Bill," said Nurse Nancy. "I'll look after you. You'll soon be as fit as a fiddle."

First she cleaned Bill's hand. It stung a bit but he was very brave.

Then Nurse Nancy put on a clean, white bandage.

Soon Builder Bill felt much better. He thanked Nurse Nancy for looking after him and went back to work.

When Nurse Nancy
had seen all the other
patients and tidied up, it
was time to go home.

What a long and busy day
it had been!

Library

At home, Nurse Nancy climbed into bed.

"All I need is a good night's sleep," she told Patch, "and in the morning, I'll be as fit as a fiddle!"

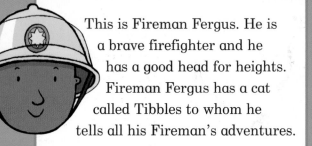

This is Fireman Fergus. He is a brave firefighter and he has a good head for heights. Fireman Fergus has a cat called Tibbles to whom he tells all his Fireman's adventures.

This is Nurse Nancy. She is always neat and tidy and she works very hard looking after the patients at Story Town Hospital.

This is Builder Bill with his yellow hard hat. Builder Bill loves to whistle. He is a very good builder, and his houses never fall down.